The Funny Ride

by Margaret Hillert

Illustrated by Józef Sumichrast

DEAR CAREGIVER,

The *Beginning-to-Read* series is a carefully written collection of classic readers you may remember from your own childhood. Each book features text comprised of common sight words to provide your child ample practice reading the words that appear most frequently in written text. The many additional details in the pictures enhance the story and offer the opportunity for you to help your child expand oral language and develop comprehension.

Begin by reading the story to your child, followed by letting him or her read familiar words and soon your child will be able to read the story independently. At each step of the way, be sure to praise your reader's efforts to build his or her confidence as an independent reader. Discuss the pictures and encourage your child to make connections between the story and his or her own life. At the end of the story, you will find reading activities and a word list that will help your child practice and strengthen beginning reading skills.

Above all, the most important part of the reading experience is to have fun and enjoy it!

Shannon Cannon

Shannon Cannon,
Literacy Consultant

Norwood House Press • P.O. Box 316598 • Chicago, Illinois 60631
For more information about Norwood House Press please visit our website at
www.norwoodhousepress.com or call 866-565-2900.

LIBRARY OF CONGRESS CATALOGING-IN-PUBLICATION DATA

Hillert, Margaret.
   The funny ride / Margaret Hillert ; illustrated by Jozef Sumichrast. —
Rev. and expanded library ed.
     p. cm. — (Beginning-to-read series)
   Summary: "When his kite lifts him above the ground, a child takes a "funny ride"
as he views what is on the ground and in the air"—provided by publisher.
   ISBN-13: 978-1-59953-149-6 (library edition : alk. paper)
   ISBN-10: 1-59953-149-6 (library edition : alk. paper) [1. Kites—Fiction.
2. Flight—Fiction.] I. Sumichrast, Jvzef., il II. Title.
PZ7.H558Fu 2008
[E]—dc22
                                        2007034733

Oh, look.
Here is something big.
I can play with it.
I can make it go up.

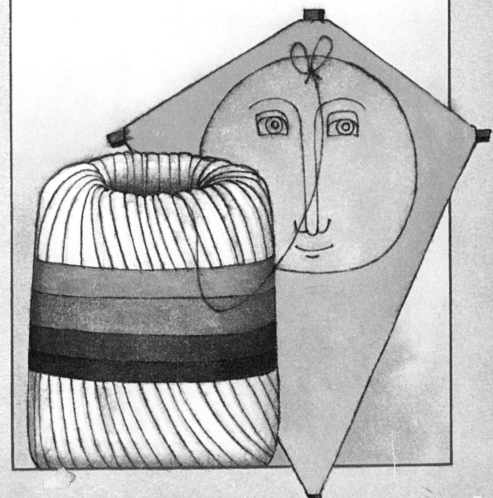

See me run.
And see it go up.
Up, up, up.
Look at it go!

Oh, my. Oh, my.
I can go up, too.
Here I go.
Up, up—and away!

Look down. Look down.
I see cars.
I see my house.
I see my mother.

Mother, Mother.
Look up here.
Look at me go.
See what I can do.

No, no.
You can not do that.
Come down here to me.
I want you.

This is fun.
It is fun up here.
Look at me go.
Away, away, away.

Now I see my school.
It is a big one,
but it looks little.

And the boys and girls
look little, too.
That is funny.

Oh, oh.
Something is up here
with me now.
Something big, big, big.
Do you like it up here?

What will you do now?
Where will you go?
I want to go, too.

Oh, what is this?
I can not see in here.
I want to get out.

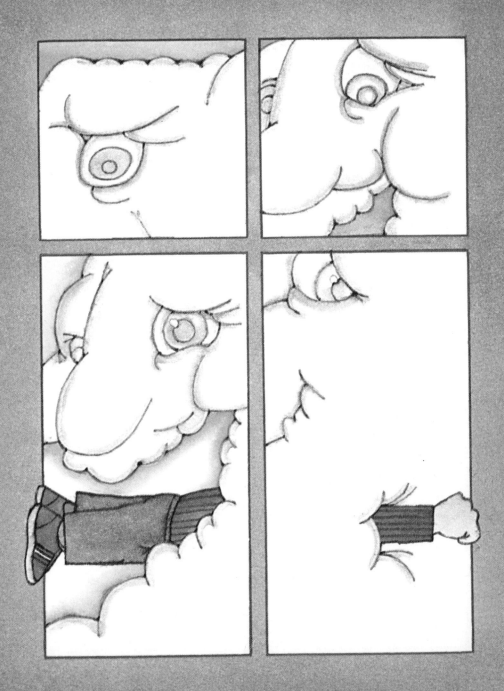

Now I am out.
But I am up, up, up.
Oh, my. Oh, my.

Look at that!
See it go down.
Down and down and down.

And now look.
I like to see this.
Red, yellow, blue.
How pretty it is!

Here is something pretty, too.
One, two, three pretty ones.
Oh, my. Oh, my.

And look at this.
See what this man can do.
He is good at it.

No, no.
Go away. Go away.
I do not want you to do this.
Look out. Look out.
This is not good for me.

Oh, oh.
Down I go.
What can I do?
Help! Help!

Mother, Mother.
Here I come.
Down,
   down,
      down.

28

Oh, my.
What a ride!
What a funny, funny ride!

The following activities support the findings of the National Reading Panel that determined the most effective components for reading instruction are: Phonemic Awareness, Phonics, Vocabulary, Fluency, and Text Comprehension.

Phonemic Awareness: Syllabication

Say the following words, clapping the syllables as you say them. Ask your child to tell you how many syllables are in each word:

funny-2	away-2	little-2	big-1	like-1
bicycle-3	popcorn-2	up-1	with-1	
something-2	holiday-3	pretty-2	school-2	
mother-2	chocolate-3	pumpkin-2	carpet-2	
table-2	chair-1	fantastic-3	remember-3	

Phonics: Syllabication

1. Write the following word parts on separate index cards. Display the syllables for each word, out of order, and help your child put them together to make words:

fun/ny	a/way	bi/cy/cle	re/mem/ber
pump/kin	fan/tas/tic	pop/corn	hol/i/day
lit/tle	pret/ty	some/thing	yel/low
pup/py	kit/ten	care/ful	fa/ther
cook/ie	pen/cil		

Vocabulary: Homophones

1. On a blank sheet of paper, make three rows by drawing two lines. Write the following story words in each row: to, too, two. Ask your child to read the words aloud. Discuss with your child that to indicates movement or action, too means also or as well, and two is the word for the number 2.

2. Read the following sentences from left to right and ask your child to point to the homophone (to, too, or two) that is being used:

I am going to the store.   Do you want to go too?
      We will buy two apples.

I like cookies, do you like them too?   I want to eat two cookies.
      We can go to the bakery to buy cookies.

My bicycle has two wheels.   My sister has a bicycle too.
      We will ride our bicycles to the park.

My class went on a trip to the museum.   The other class went too.
      There were so many kids, we had to take two buses.

3. Ask your child to make statements and ask questions using the different homophones as you point to the correct choice for each sentence.

Fluency: Choral Reading

1. Reread the story with your child at least two more times while your child tracks the print by running a finger under the words as they are read. Ask your child to read the words he or she knows with you.

2. Reread the story aloud together. Be careful to read at a rate that your child can keep up with.

3. Repeat choral reading and allow your child to be the lead reader and ask him or her to change from a whisper to a loud voice while you follow along and change your voice.

Text Comprehension: Discussion Time

1. Ask your child to retell the sequence of events in the story.

2. To check comprehension, ask your child the following questions:

   • What is the funny ride in the story?

   • Which parts of the story could really happen?

   • Which parts of the story could not really happen?

   • What made the boy in the story go down? How do you think he felt when that happened?

WORD LIST

***The Funny Ride* uses the 67 words listed below.** This list can be used to practice reading the words that appear in the text. You may wish to write the words on index cards and use them to help your child build automatic word recognition. Regular practice with these words will enhance your child's fluency in reading connected text.

a	for	like	play	up
am	fun	little	pretty	
and	funny	look(s)		want
at			red	what
away	get	make	ride	where
	girls	man	run	will
big	go	me		with
blue	good	mother	school	
boys		my	see	yellow
but	he		something	you
	help	no		
can	here	not	that	
cars	house	now	the	
come	how		this	
		oh	three	
do	I	one(s)	to	
down	in	out	too	
	is		two	
	it			

ABOUT THE AUTHOR Margaret Hillert has written over 80 books for children who are just learning to read. Her books have been translated into many different languages and over a million children throughout the world have read her books. She first started writing poetry as a child and has continued to write for children and adults throughout her life. A first grade teacher for 34 years, Margaret is now retired from teaching and lives in Michigan where she likes to write, take walks in the morning, and care for her three cats.

Photograph by Glenna Washburn

ABOUT THE ADVISER Shannon Cannon contributed the activities pages that appear in this book. Shannon serves as a literacy consultant and provides staff development to help improve reading instruction. She is a frequent presenter at educational conferences and workshops. Prior to this she worked as an elementary school teacher and as president of a curriculum publishing company.